Pocketful of Gold

by Ben Butterworth
Illustrated by Wayne Anderson

Once upon a time
there was a King who wanted to find
an honest man.
He wanted to find an honest man to
look after all the gold in his kingdom.
He went to see Simon, his wise man.

"Simon," said the King.
"I want to find an honest man
to look after all the gold
in my kingdom.
How shall I find one?"

3

"That's easy," said Simon.
"I will find you an honest man."

"You sit on the throne," said Simon.
"I shall send all the people
who want to look after the gold
through a long empty room."

"I do not see what good that will do,"
said the King.
"Wait and see," said Simon.

The first man came.
Simon sent him through
the long, empty room, and
he came to the King.

"Now dance for the King,"
said Simon.

"No! No! I don't want to!"
said the first man.

The second man came.
Simon sent him through
the long empty room, and
he came to the King.

"Now dance for the King,"
said Simon.

"No! No! I don't want to!"
said the second man.

Lots of men came.
They all went through
the long, empty room, and
they all said they didn't want
to dance for the King.

Then another man came.
Simon sent him through
the long, empty room, and
he came to the King.
"Now dance for the King," said Simon.

"I will try," said the man
and he danced.

"This is your honest man," said Simon.
"How do you know that?"
asked the King.

"There was one thing in the long,
empty room," Simon said.
"I put a sack full of gold in there."

"The other men would not dance
because they had taken some gold.
You would have heard it jingling
in their pockets if they had danced."